For Lynn Rowland with many thanks – SG
For Tiziana – JB-B

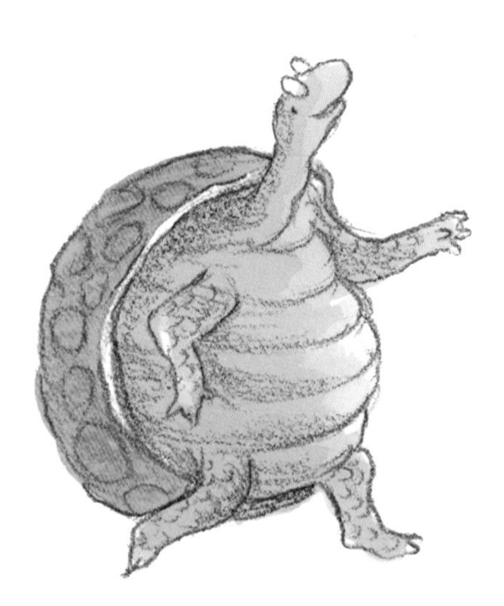

First published in Great Britain in 1999 by Bloomsbury Publishing Plc
38 Soho Square, London W1V 5DF

A CIP catalogue record for this book is available from the British Library.
ISBN 0 7475 3650 3

Designed by Dawn Apperley

Printed in Dubai by Oriental Press

1 3 5 7 9 10 8 6 4 2

Aesop's Fables for the Very Young

The Hare and the Tortoise

And Other Animal Stories

Sally Grindley and John Bendall-Brunello

INTRODUCTION

Aesop has become a household name – most obviously for his fables, but also for the expressions that we use every day: 'sour grapes', 'a wolf in sheep's clothing', 'the boy who cried wolf', 'don't count your chickens before they are hatched', which almost certainly spring from his original fables. It is ironic therefore that we know so little about somebody who has had such an influence over the centuries. We think that he was Greek, and lived in the Sixth century BC. We think that he was probably a slave. Some say that he was thrown off a cliff at Delphi because of his stories, others that he was deformed in some way. And others say that he never existed at all...

Whatever the truth is, there can be no doubt that these stories of cunning and wit, of morality and lessons of character have enormous appeal. And in this younger picture book format we hope to broaden the audience for Aesop (whoever he was) and his fables. Sally Grindley's re-tellings race along with humour and verve, perfectly complemented by John Bendall-Brunello's lively illustrations. A book that we hope will be treasured, read and re-read for generations to come.

Contents

The Hare and the Tortoise

One hot, sunny day, a hare was lazing on a grassy bank when he saw a tortoise walking slowly by. The hare snickered, then he sniggered, then he snorted, then he couldn't help himself and burst out laughing – '*TEE-HEE-HEE! HA-HA-HA!*'

The tortoise stopped and gazed at the hare. 'What's so funny?' she asked. 'It's your feet,' said the hare. 'They're so short – *TEE-HEE-HEE!* And you're so slow – *HA-HA-HA!* Do you ever arrive where you're going?'

The tortoise blinked thoughtfully and said, 'I may be slow, but I will beat you in a race.'

The hare couldn't believe his great big ears and burst out laughing again. 'What are you going to do, grow wings?' he giggled. 'All right, we'll meet here tomorrow morning. Make sure you eat your spinach – *HA-HA-HA!*'

With that, the hare leapt away to show how fast he was while the tortoise plodded on her way.

Bright and early the next morning, the hare and the tortoise lined up to begin their race. *READY, STEADY, GO!*

The hare shot off – *WHOOSH!* – and was quickly out of sight.

The tortoise set off at her usual pace – *PLOD, PLOD, PLOD.* She didn't stop to eat, she didn't stop to drink, she didn't stop to rest, she kept on going – *PLOD, PLOD, PLOD.*

The hare stopped to eat. The hare stopped to drink. The hare stopped to rest. 'Plenty of time,' he said. '*HA-HA-HA!* A tortoise can't beat a hare!' – and he soon fell fast asleep.

PLOD, PLOD, PLOD – the tortoise was closing the gap. *SNORE! SNORE!* – the tortoise was passing the hare. *PLOD, PLOD, PLOD* – the tortoise could see the finishing line.

The hare woke up and looked back down the path. 'Plenty of time,' he said. '*TEE-HEE-HEE!* She must be miles behind!'

But who was that in front of him? Whose short feet were crossing the finishing line?

'Wait!' yelled the hare. 'Too late,' said the tortoise, and she plodded on her way.

The Fox and the Grapes

Once upon a time, a very hungry fox was looking for food, when he saw the most enormous bunch of fat grapes hanging from a trellis.

O, how his eyes grew as big as saucers! O, how his tummy rumbled and his mouth watered!

'I must have those grapes,' panted the fox.

He leapt as high as he could, but he couldn't reach even the lowest hanging grape.

He stood on his hind legs on a wall, but the grapes dangled tantalisingly just above his nose, close enough to sniff but not close enough to bite.

‘I’ll get those grapes if it’s the last thing I do,’ he snapped.

He tried climbing up the trellis, but a rose tree grew there as well as the vine. ‘Ow, ow, ow!’ he yelped as he trod on one thorn after another. He jumped onto the grass and licked his wounds.

Then the fox grabbed a stick in his mouth and tried knocking the grapes down. Two of them came free. They fell to the ground. He leapt after them and tried to catch them, just as they rolled down a drain.

The fox couldn’t believe his bad luck. He looked at the grapes one last time, then sloped away. ‘I bet they tasted horrible, anyway,’ he declared.

The Hare and the Hound

A hound was bounding across a field one day when he startled a hare lazing in the sun. The hare raced away, yelping with fear – 'YELP, YELP, HELP!' The hound chased after her snapping at her heels and barking excitedly – 'WOOF, WOOF, FOOD!' They ran this way and that, dashing here, darting there. But after a while the hound gave up the chase and sat and washed his paws.

A young boy, seeing him stop, laughed at him and said, 'That little hare is obviously a much better runner than you.'

The hound stopped washing and looked scornfully at the boy.

'You obviously haven't noticed an important difference between us: I was only running for my dinner. She was running for her life.'

The Lion and the Mouse

One hot summer's day, a mouse stepped lightly across a lion's nose, thinking it was an unusually soft piece of ground.

The lion's paw stopped the mouse in her tracks and pinned her down by the tail. 'You woke me up, and now I'm hungry,' roared the lion, licking his lips and flexing his claws.

The mouse was terrified. 'Please let me go,' she squealed. 'I promise to help you if ever you are in trouble.'

The lion looked at the mouse and laughed his head off. 'Do you really think that you, a mere mouse, could ever help me, king of all beasts?' He laughed again, and was so amused at the idea of a mouse helping him that he let her go.

Some weeks later, the lion was caught in a trap set by hunters. A net made of strong rope fell over his head and was pulled tight round him. The lion roared a mighty roar – R - O - A - R! – and struggled to free himself. But the more he struggled, the more tied up in the net he became.
R - O - A - R! he roared, angrily.

The mouse heard the lion roar. She remembered her promise and ran to find him. When she saw how he was caught, she began to gnaw at the rope with her sharp teeth.

'You'll never do it,' growled the lion. 'A little thing like you.'

'You'll be surprised,' said the mouse.

She went on gnawing, hour after hour, not stopping to rest, until at last she had made a hole big enough for the lion to crawl out.

'Never judge a thing by its size,' said the mouse, and she scampered away, leaving the lion lost for words.

The Fox and the Crow

Early one morning a crow plucked a big, fat, juicy worm from the ground and flew up into a tree with it. A passing fox saw her and determined to have the worm for breakfast. He quickly thought up a plan while the crow perched on a branch wondering which end of the worm to eat first.

'What a handsome bird is the crow!' declared the fox, loudly.

The crow, hearing the fox's words, fluttered her wings modestly.

'Her shape is so beautiful and her colouring magnificent!' continued the fox. The crow stretched her neck and proudly stuck out her chest.

'Oh, if only her voice were just as beautiful then she would deserve to be crowned Queen of the Birds!' said the fox, craftily.

The crow was annoyed that the fox didn't value her voice. 'CAW, CAW, CAW!' she cawed. 'There's nothing wrong with my –' As she opened her beak, the worm dropped straight into the fox's open mouth.

'My good crow,' said the fox, smugly, when he had swallowed the worm, 'there's nothing wrong with your voice, but there's plenty wrong with your brain.'

The Ants and the Grasshopper

All summer long the ants were busy. They built their nests, they laid their eggs, they cut up leaves and picked up crumbs, and they collected grain to put in their food store for the long winter days ahead – work, work, work, work, work.

And all summer long a grasshopper sat in the grass, watching the working ants, and singing loudly. He sang quick songs and slow songs, noisy songs and quiet songs, funny songs and sad songs – sing, sing, sing, sing, sing.

When autumn came, the ants busily dried out grain they had collected during the summer. Backwards and forwards they scurried, carrying pieces of grain to and from their nest.

Then winter came. The grasshopper, weak with hunger, crawled up to the ants and begged, ‘Spare a little food for a poor, starving creature.’

The ants stopped in their tracks and asked,
‘Why didn’t you store food for yourself in the summer?’

The grasshopper replied, ‘Oh, I was far too busy singing.’

The ants couldn’t believe their ears. They laughed at him scornfully and said, ‘If you were foolish enough to sing all summer, then you must dance to bed with an empty belly in the winter.’

With that they bade him good day and scuttled back to work.

The Jackdaw and the Doves

One winter's day, a hungry jackdaw watched a family of doves pecking happily at some seed the farmer had put out for them. 'Cor!' he squawked. 'I want some of that!' Luckily for him, a pot of white paint had been left in the garden with the lid off. He flew down to it, dipped in a wing, and painted himself white all over.

Then he flew over to the doves and mingled with them. As long as he was silent, the doves thought he was one of them and he was able to eat as much as he wanted.

But one day the jackdaw forgot himself and began to chatter. 'Lovely grub this, isn't it?' he said. 'Cor, you don't know how lucky you are to have humans feeding you every day.' The doves looked at him in horror. 'Imposter!' they shrilled. 'You're not one of us!' They pecked at him with their beaks and drove him away.

Smoothing his ruffled feathers, the jackdaw flew back to his own family and friends. 'I'm back,' he squawked. 'Have you missed me?' They took one look at him and screeched, 'Intruder! You're not one of us. Get away from here.' They too pecked at him with their beaks and drove him away.

The poor jackdaw had to live all on his own until he had grown new feathers and could be himself again.

The Mice in Council

One evening, a large family of mice gathered together for a meeting under the floorboards of a house.

'We have called this meeting,' announced one mouse, 'to find a way to outsmart our enemy, the cat.'

'If only we knew when he was coming,' said another mouse, 'he might not catch so many of us.'

'Has anyone got any ideas?' asked the third mouse.

The mice all started talking at once and came up with one idea after another.

‘I’ve got a good idea,’ squeaked one little mouse. ‘We could tie a bell round his neck. When we hear it tinkling we’ll know he’s coming and can run away and hide.’

The other mice cheered loudly at this idea and patted the little mouse on the head.

‘Well, then,’ said the first mouse. ‘There’s only one last thing to be decided. Who is going to tie the bell round the cat’s neck?’

The mice all looked at each other in horror. ‘Tie the bell round the cat’s neck! Not me!’ they squeaked. ‘Not me, not me, not me!’

The meeting closed with no agreement on any further action.

The Fox and the Goat

A fox was racing along one day when he fell down a well – WHOOPS! He tried and tried but he could not get out again.

A little while later, a very thirsty goat came to the same well. He looked down and saw the fox. 'What's the water like?' he bleated.

The fox put on a smiley face. 'It's the most delicious water I have ever tasted in my life. Come and try some.'

The goat didn't need to be told twice. He leapt straight in and gulped down as much water as he could until his thirst was quenched.

'The only problem is,' said the fox, as the goat stood licking his lips, 'I think we might be stuck here.'

The goat looked round the well and up at the steep walls and began to bleat miserably.

'I have a very clever plan, though,' said the fox, 'to help us both escape.'

The goat listened eagerly. He didn't want to be stuck down the well forever.

The fox continued. 'If you stretch your front legs up the side of the well as far as they will go and bend your head down, I will run up your back and leap out over the top. Then I will help you out.'

The goat agreed straightaway. He got himself into position, lowered his head, and stood quite still as the fox ran up his back, held on to his horns and hauled himself out of the well.

When the goat raised his head again, he saw the fox waving goodbye.

'Hey!' he bleated. 'Where are you going? You promised to help me out.'

The fox leaned over the wall and said, 'You are a foolish fellow. If you had as many brains in your head as you have hairs in your beard, you would never have jumped into the well in the first place without checking how you were going to get out. I am afraid I cannot help you.'

With that, the fox skipped away and left the goat to his fate.

The Peacock and the Crane

A peacock strutted into a garden and opened his tail as wide as he could. Then he moved to a spot where the light would shine right on him, and stood there in all his splendour thinking how wonderful he must look. When a crane passed by, the peacock looked at him and sneered. 'Where were you when the colours were given out? Here am I, dressed like a king in gold and purple and all the colours of the rainbow, and there you are clothed from head to toe in nothing but drab.'